Other books by Denver Day

Pizza Noir No. 1: "Catch as Catch Can" (2014)

Hipster Bricks: The Cost of Doing Business (2016)

Pizza Noir No. 3: "Pie in the Sky" (2017)

The Only Game in Town (c. 2018)

Alpha Taxonomy

Alpha Taxonomy

Pizza Noir No. 2

Denver Day

Second Edition
Story by Denver Day
One, Otto, editor & publisher
Braswell Business Communications Services Inc., printer
cover and text printed on 100% post-consumer fiber stock from New
Leaf Paper©

Literature is art, all dharma is fire, and this copy of *Pizza Noir
No. 2 - Alpha Taxonomy* is yours to keep.
The *Pizza Noir* series is a work of fiction cut from whole cloth,
none of the events occurred and I invented the characters
notwithstanding arguments from wardens and werewolves.

Rev. date: January 2018

To order additional copies of the book contact:
Braswell Business Communications Services Inc.
1-518-400-2729
www.fusepowder.com
www.denverday.com

Table of Contents

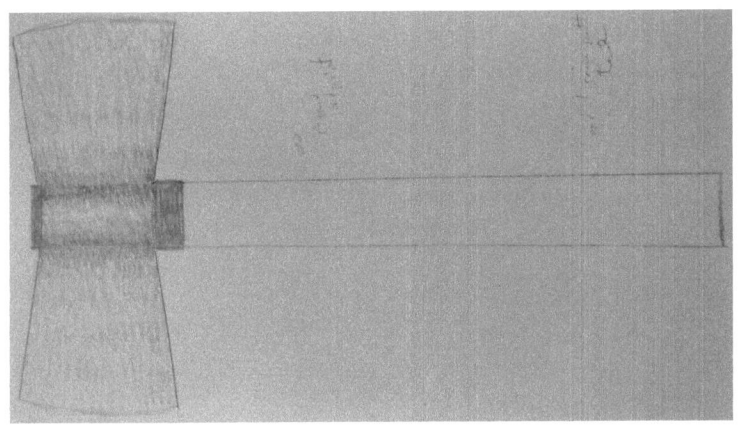

New Monday

When detective Scott Smith arrived at his desk on Monday morning, there was a note from a detective named Thompson. Rick Thompson, a colleague in the homicide division, asking after any progress on the Tina Santos case. Santos had been a girlfriend of Thompson's after some fashion.

Smith had ten years with the Seattle city force before coming to the Washington State

Police thirteen months back. He did not think of himself as green but nobody needs ten years to see that Thompson's primary investigation had moved beyond the pale of normal police work.

R. Thompson's in-good-faith efforts at investigating the local editions of a rash of interstate nightclub stripper killings had been grossly unsuccessful, but it was not his fault. Substantively the case had waxed supernatural. Thompson could not just let it go but there was nothing firm to hang on to, so his position was awkward. It was a messy case that would probably never be squared away, and Smith admitted to himself, he was glad it was not his.

The Santos case was an axe murder. It

was not boring work, nevertheless Smith was glad Newton's laws and the life sciences had remained intact for him. So far.

Ms. Santos' band had a regular gig at a hotel lounge frequented by some of Thompson's suspects in the October 11 homicide cluster. Thompson had been involved sexually with Santos in the past week, which of course had turned out to be Santos' last week ever.

In addition to his being swamped with science-fiction-come-fact, Thompson's conflict of interest was another reason for Smith's drawing the Santos case. When they talked on Saturday, Thompson recommended monitoring the regular crowd at the hotel where her jazz group was the house act. The woman had been a former Forest Ranger, notable in part because she was killed with her own axe.

Fifty-six hours earlier the bass player had found the body with a single well-angled edge-end blow to the top of her skull. Santos had been an attractive woman about five-feet-six-inches tall with neck-length, almost-black straight hair. She was not sexually assaulted during the crime, the Pierce County coroner told.

Smith had met the surviving members of Santos' band on Saturday and spent all of Saturday evening at that hotel lounge. It was an exceedingly difficult emotional time for the musicians however they had a strong, natural compulsion to persist, which served them as a strong coping mechanism. They knew the detective was there to parse the crowd for suspects, and the band played on.

Frequently, the patrons were transient business-class types, and the lounge received intermittent traffic from the strip club up the block. He did not, at a blush, see any true standouts. A couple of freelancers, shortly after midnight, came in and sat at the bar until close. Smith tarried until about three.

On Sunday afternoon Smith followed up on a tip from the band, a man and a woman involved in an intermittent tryst with Santos. They were academic types and fair-weather friends of hers evidently, with a residential address at a bungalow downtown. The woman answered the door holding a broom. She looked down at the badge that hung from his neck on a lanyard.

She held out her hand. "Hello. May I help you sir?" politely, she queried.

"My name is Scott Smith of the state police. Tacoma office, homicide division," he answered. "Tina Santos was killed Friday night and I am investigating her death."

He looked into her eyes. They widened for a moment. With one foot she stepped back lightly, her handshake unmet.

"I'm sorry. I can see that you are upset. It is important that I ask you some questions," he went on, "because you knew the victim."

The woman invited him in briskly. She

looked genuinely disturbed by the bad news. She caught her breath in about five minutes and introduced herself as Daisy Wilson. She said her housemate's name was Skip Foster, Professor Skip Foster who was not present, having gone to his office on campus. She offered tea and they sat on the couch in the sunlit den while the woman described her and Skip Foster's friendship with Tina Santos.

About three years ago, Foster and Wilson had met Santos on campus, where Skip is an associate professor, when Daisy was still an undergraduate, she said. They were wine buddies. She teared-up as she talked. Same as the band, Wilson was unable to think of who or why anyone would want to harm the victim. By all accounts including Thompson's, Santos was viewed as an upright, pleasant, intelligent woman who suffered no earned antagonists.

It does not shock the conscience of the community if a criminal, bridge dweller, or addict meets a violent end; it is unlikely for actual normal people to be murdered with an axe. The uniform consensus among the people who knew her was, the killing was out of hat because Santos was clean, picture perfect. At face value, the bewilderment of the victim's friends and colleagues looked legitimate.

Looking For Hotspots

It was a short trip from the bungalow to
the campus art building where S. Foster's
work space was cluttered with art in
progress and its implements. Books and
charts, shelves, easels, paint, chalk, ink,
stain, and plumes of all colors. Cans,
chemicals, lumber, boxes, buckets, crates,
paper, cardboard, newsprint, canvas, tarp,
tape, and you name it. Several fans guided

the central studio's chemical-heavy air. All windows were open.

There were no clocks on the walls. The doors to most of the smaller dwellings, offices, and classrooms were closed. Some had been long painted over. Some of the few open ones led to stuffed closets, or whole rooms with clutter up to the ceiling. Some doors had evolved from their hinges toward more novel applications.

In exception to reasonable expectations that undergraduates cannot be found on campus on Sundays, a couple of students helped Foster with the practically endless task of cleaning and organizing. The professor stood in front of a large plastic tub sink, rinsing out brushes and cans and setting them up to dry on a towel-covered drafting table.

He looked up when Smith entered the studio. Realizing he did not recognize his visitor, he shut off the faucet, set down his work, and dried his hands on a towel hanging from the backboard of the sink.

Smith introduced himself and related to the professor his conversation with Daisy Wilson. Foster suggested they continue theirs outside. The men walked out together. He put the same questions to the professor:

"Did she have any real debts..."

"Were there any jilted lovers..."

"Are you privy to any private habits or personal walks that might be relevant..."

"Is there anything you can think of, anything at all, that may help move this investigation forward..."

"Professor..." he nudged. The would-be suspect was candid if not glib.

"Well, her band played, or rather plays regularly at a hotel lounge. But that's no mystery," he answered first. "You must know that much by now."

"The bass player found the body," Smith said. "Your input is important because the three of you were close. Please tell me more."

"No I'm at a loss. She's well liked, competent, friendly, disarming, mindful," he said. "No one would have legitimate reason.

Ever. And because she is a sharp, observant, canny former wilderness firefighter, frankly I am surprised to hear anyone was able to attack her without being made and shut down by her."

"When is the last time you or Daisy saw Ms. Santos?" Smith asked.

"Last weekend. The Friday before last. It was one of her band's nights off," he said. "The three of us met at our favorite pub."

"What is it called?" the detective asked.

"Kelly Sammys," Foster answered.

"Did she mention about anything new, unusual, or different? Was there anything out of the ordinary. Anything of the like," lightly Smith further pressed.

"No," he answered, he paused. "No."

"What did you all talk about at your last meeting?" Smith continued.

The professor's eyes rolled up as he recalled historical conversations. "Work, more or less. The usual. My work. Her work. Daisy's work. Mostly art, artists, music, and musicians. Off-duty shop talk. Our work is common ground for us. We love to do it and we love to talk about it. As far as actual dialog, it's generally all we ever talk about."

"What does Daisy do?" Smith asked.

"Daisy's a chef at a couple of restaurants in the area," the professor answered.

"Were you and Daisy sexually involved with Ms. Santos?" the detective asked.

"We've had our moments," he answered with mixed emotions, but steadily. "More importantly, Tina is family to us. Pretty soon after Daisy and I got together, we met her at Kelly Sammys which is always thick with graduate students and faculty, colleagues and friends, and within walking distance of this office and our apartment and Daisy's jobs. Tina basically kept a book there and was a regular. We became fast friends and it stuck."

First thing Monday morning, Smith went for another look at the Santos residence.

The bedroom of her rented apartment was orderly and her vanities were practical. Her trappings were simple woven bracelets, beachwear hemp stuff, turquoise and the like.

Sensible, subtle things. Her horns, the tools of her trade, were there. Along with her vehicle and an impressive collection of outdoor sporting gear, her musical instruments may have been the estate's only real property.

Nothing was noticeably missing, and the windows, doors, and all of their latches were intact. The dwelling had not been burgled during the crime. The killer did not apparently break in.

He, she, or it either was invited in, possessed a key, used an unsecured egress, or got a foot in the door and pushed through Santos. The body was in the den, well clear of both the apartment's front and back doors.

Judging by the heaviest blood marks on the floor, and the spatter fanning out from that focus, she bled out and died where she was attacked between the couch and the T.V.

The detective walked the rooms. She had plants but no roommates and no pets. The spare bedroom was used to store her musical and outdoors gear and other hardware. Smith opened up the cases and looked at her saxes. She had three very nice horns, well worn but maintained perfectly. He returned to her bedroom, sat on the bed, and thought about the scope of her regular audience.

He went back to the couch in the den and sat, looking toward the front door. From a low table before him he picked up the remote television control and switched on the set. The volume was turned down and the dial was tuned to an all-weather channel.

He locked the front door, went outside, and knocked on the doors of neighboring apartments. Only one knock was answered, by a middle-aged lady two doors down. The woman said she had moved in six weeks ago, and only spoken brief courtesies, in passing, to Santos, who she presumed was a "moon-lighting graduate student of some sort or another."

Smith walked to the parking lot and unlocked Santos' compact sedan. In and out, the car was clean, economical, and practical. Nothing was in the glove box except an owner's manual and an insurance document, and the trunk was empty but for a jack and

spare tire. All neat as a pin, with
Washington state plates. He walked the
perimeter of the apartment complex which
was surrounded by Garry oak trees, though
in all directions none of it was far from the
asphalt and concrete of neighboring retail
and residential properties.

Santos' next of kin was an aunt on the
East Coast, where the body would be shipped
once Smith authorized its release. The
coroner's report was clear and thorough and
Smith could not think of any good reason,
save for forensic bait, why he should retain
the body come next week.

Do, Re....

The noon hour Monday found Smith staring at his office desk and a blank notepad. There was Foster, and Wilson, and the musicians. And the aunt back east. Hell there was even Thompson.

S. Foster was a tartan velvet master of fine arts. The man read to the detective a story that was cool, practical, and thoughtful. The detective understood the professor came across as an open book because such a presentation was his intent, although evidently, the man was also honestly and sufficiently preoccupied with the trappings of his world and probably readily accessible to any person who spoke his language. The house of cards Foster presented was all that Smith had to work with for the moment and his mere depth was grounds for plausible suspicion; Such is the forensic nature of professional thinkers, the detective thought. Like plants in their rote mannerisms, or like losing politicians tending to comport themselves with a certain transcending veracity.

Objectively, the professor's best alibi was his demonstrated reasonability. And as Foster, so Wilson, possibly. And the band?

Denver Day

Professional musicians. A busy lot of working artisans, a tight business unit all of whom cited their historically usually-successful policy against inter-member romantic affairs. Ostensibly, they were all too busy with their colorful careers and lives to have a hazardous side job as an axe murderer. And they all had similar dispositions as Santos, that is not befitting any obvious nut-job profile, personality-wise. Their alibis were as strong as the professor's, though equally self-referential.

As innocent as it does not sound, detective Thompson, lieutenant Dan MacKinney, and the Pierce County Coroner Dixie Thompson who is detective Thompson's ex-wife, were all up that morning at the

DPS tow lot burning an ambulance. The former first-response vehicle was connected to the interstate crime spree which had most recently culminated, some thirty-six hours ago, in a deadly shootout at a nearby warehouse parking lot. The warehouse scene was no less than a proper riot which featured police-involved shootings, multiple dead civilians, and worse. What's more, an investigator from Oakland (the chief of police, no joke), having been involved with the October 11 homicide investigations in his own jurisdiction, had driven all the way to Tacoma to help destroy the ambulance.

Rick Thompson himself had gunned down multiple perpetrators during Saturday night's fiasco. His colleague certainly had some rough edges, but Smith's observations over the past year found Thompson's inner workings to be all right. Undeniably, Thompson was an effective investigator, an ethical peace officer, and a man generally simple and divorced. His were not the requisites of an axe murderer. Oppositely, in fact, Thompson was instead wired to destroy evidence for the safety of the citizens of Washington state, and to skillfully kill anyone or anything necessary toward that end, in the due course of a public melee. The man simply was not that dark or complex, and his jar did not contain any recipes for a cowardly ambush on a friend or casual lover.

For the sake of being thorough, detective

Smith believed he needed an in-person conversation with Santos' aunt. He knew traveling to Philadelphia and back would be a long trip for what probably would be a thirty-minute interview with an old lady in a straw hat, but at least the health benefits of a temporary change in scenery would justify the effort.

He decided to take a lunch at Kelly Sammys. It was an Irish tavern of brass and dark wood. The inside was buzzing with the lightness of a beery, lunching university crowd. He sat alone at the end of the bar, and set his badge down next to his wallet to give a slightly increased edge to his presence. A group of students walked in behind him, took one of the large tables, and

Denver Day

ordered a round of burritos and several pitchers of beer. Smith was handed a menu and ordered a bean burger and soda. His food arrived within ten minutes. The barkeep was busy but Smith asked anyway:

"Do you know Tina Santos?"

"Yep," he answered.

"She was murdered in her apartment Friday night," Smith said.

With a pencil behind one ear, a short-order pad in one hand and his other on a beer tap, the barman looked up and studied the detective more thoroughly. "Are you a policeman?" he asked.

"Yes I am. And I am investigating her death. How well did you know her?" Smith

34

asked.

"As a regular and a welcome patron here," he answered. "A very nice lady."

"Did she have any new friends, or boyfriends, or lovers? I can't find anybody to give me any reason why anyone would harm her," Smith said. "Not any of her regular, or known, acquaintances anyway."

"Not as far as I saw. She kept to her crowd, like musician types," the bartender said. Smith studied him. The dude was in his late thirties or early forties, of a medium build with short dark hair and blue eyes, wearing jeans and a brown short-sleeved Kelly Sammys knit shirt.

"What about Daisy Wilson and Skip

Foster?" Smith asked.

"Part of Tina's circle," he answered, "a local artist and restaurateur."

"Do you know if the professor and his wife ever had any sort of romantic relationship with the victim?" Smith asked.

"I can't speak for what goes on behind closed doors, officer," the man said, as he rung up another pitcher. "But they were obviously dear friends. Tina's crowd are all good people and always welcome here."

It was about two-thirty as Smith finished up his bean burger and soda, paid his bill, and returned to his office. He telephoned Santos' aunt, who granted his request to interview her in the coming days. The detective booked a red-eye departure for tomorrow morning, and a Wednesday night return. The line double-chirped as he hung it up, indicating an in-house call:

"They fished a musician out of Budd Inlet this morning," lieutenant MacKinney announced. With that, Smith turned on his heel and drove south on I-5 to Olympia's old downtown district.

Wet Matches

Smith pulled up to the Olympia police

headquarters and walked inside. After a
short conversation with the front desk and a
short wait while she used the phone, he took
directions for the Port of Olympia Marine
Terminal, a few blocks north.

As he approached, he saw yellow police
tape strung up in the yard, leading to his
contact detective David Wallace of the
Olympia police department. The men shook
hands.

"Drowning?" he asked.

"I don't think so," Wallace snorted.
"Although some or another volume of her
flesh probably did end up in the Sound."

Wallace looked up and waved at a
Thurston County Sheriff's Office vehicle

driving away. The two detectives were left alone in the industrial lot. "A woman in her late twenties last seen by friends on Saturday night at a downtown bar a few blocks away," Wallace said.

"She was a musician, I hear tell," Smith remarked.

"Yeah, part of some outfit gigging at the bar which was her last known location," the man said. "I've known MacKinney for some years. He said you're on a case that may be related. What's up?"

"OK. Female saxophone player, mid-thirties, in the regular lounge band at a hotel in Tacoma. She was a retired firefighter and an earthy girl with zero enemies, killed at home with her own axe. The bass player found her Friday night," Smith said, "Name's Tina Santos."

"Are you watching anybody who's worth it?" Wallace asked.

"All of her associates' noses are clean, at least at a glance. Then again so was hers, and look where it got her," Smith said. "There is the band to consider and under the circumstances, the bass player particularly, but they're simply not ticking. Every one of them is an ice cold fish. I am more cautious about a pair of her ex-lovers but they're also cool to the touch, frankly."

"Hmm," Wallace grunted, beginning another swing at *quid pro quo*. "Late

Saturday, on foot just a few blocks from here, this woman left the establishment where her last show was. You might have seen the venue on your way here. She lived nearby. All this re-developed downtown district is within walking distance, including our police station." He pointed south.

"None of her people even saw the need to report her as missing and it turns out she was only gone one day and one night before we got a call from port personnel here. They found her back there in the cargo storage area," he said. "Or, what was left of her."

Wallace led the way into the maze-like array of cargo containers and palates stacked well above their heads. Several yards into a doglegging path, Wallace pointed down at bloodstains on the ground.

"She was mulched here. Katherine Wells. Twenty-nine years young." Wallace said. "Something with both blunt and sharp surfaces. Pieces of her clothing, for example, evidence the bite of an edged instrument. Likely an axe but it hasn't turned up, maybe it's in the water. What of her that was not minced or severed was bludgeoned to a pulp with a blunt end. The human remains we have salvaged here were transported to the Thurston County coroner."

They drove several miles from the scene to the coroner's office. The salvaged pieces of Wells' body had been placed in an approximately correct relative table arrangement in an effort to sort out what was what. There was male ejaculate within, evidencing recent intercourse. The sex evidently happened before she was eviscerated but the coroner couldn't tell if it had been consensual.

Smith thanked Wallace for his time, information, and access to the crime scene, and made his way back up to Tacoma.

Two axe murders of female musicians on the same weekend within thirty miles of each other. By the time Smith would return from the Commonwealth of Pennsylvania, he figured, after taking all initial statements from Wells' people, Wallace might have some new leads.

S. Smith returned to his office by way of

his apartment where he packed a travel bag. He also built a sandwich for local use and was back at the station by five o'clock.

He looked again at the results of the background checks on Foster and Wilson. In Washington state, the professor had nothing darker than a moving violation and Wilson had no apparent criminal history at all. Santos' musician friends had a smattering of sophomoric stuff like public drunkenness and reckless driving but none of it was modern.

The band had drawn straws to see who would go check on her when she did not receive their telephony as planned. The bass player who discovered Santos' body had a sensible alibi. None of Santos' known associates had any apparent turpitudinous documented history or *modus operandi*. Smith believed, correctly, that all easy money was eliminated from his investigation and he was now forced to rely on the haystack parsing of every swinging dick in the Pacific Northwest. And now, there was reason to suspect a mobile recidivist.

Determining instead to dine from one of Wilson's kitchens, he stowed the PB&J in a desk drawer.

Faith in Lovers

Wilson was a prep cook at a four star

situation in the campus district. She also worked an evening shift as an expediter at a nearby grill. Smith in the latter sat at a small booth, near a central bar that protruded from one of the entries to the kitchen. The interior was all timber, maple and airy with high ceilings compared with the nookish mahogany of Kelly Sammys. The room was flooded with solicitous aromas and the smokes of a busy supper's kitchen, waving from the back of the house to negotiate with tobaccos, wines, Scotches, ales, and various musks of the patronage. He ordered soup and baked potato.

The bar staff directly walked all food orders given at the bar to Wilson's window on the line. Several times he glimpsed her through kitchen doors. She walked up to him as he took his last bite, to ask after his meal. The restaurant was busy, she'd been preoccupied, and he thought she hadn't seen him.

"I'm flying to visit Tina's aunt in Philadelphia," he said.

She considered his words with a funny look on her face. She knew, she said, Tina did not have much for blood relatives or in-laws because she was an only child, never married, and both her parents had been dead for decades. She asked the detective to inform aunt Jan, of hers and Skip's offer for assistance, such as with the disposal of Santos' estate or other in-kind support to the family.

Denver Day

"Basically, if necessary, we can take care of it all," she said. "But right now, I need to be back to the kitchen, Mr. Smith. Please be in touch."

The detective parked at Seattle-Tacoma International Airport at three forty-five, checking no baggage. About half-past four his flight left on time and he switched planes in Chicago at lunch. On a rainy I-95 in an airport rental, by three o'clock local time he was en route to his hotel room.

In a hot shower he lathered away the accumulating travel sediment, ironed a pair of khaki cargo pants and a collared beach shirt, and lay on the hotel bed to let his spine decompress for a few minutes. He phoned Santos' aunt to confirm their appointment that evening.

Come five o'clock he drove the rental a few more miles up the interstate. It was not far to the woman's home on the southern side of the downtown Center City district. He parked down the block, walked to the address, rang the bell, and she opened the door within seconds.

Janice Allison. Smith felt not guilty at being somehow surprised, she was pleasant and modestly attractive. He'd expected her to be elderly. She wasn't.

Ms. Allison told him she was thirty-nine, Santos' father's sister's daughter, so not an aunt to Santos but a cousin, in fact. The woman invited Smith inside a decades-old, well-preserved wooden house bordered on each side by similar ones. She offered coffee and the detective declined in lieu of green tea, which she cheerfully provided. They sat. She wanted to know what happened. He gave her the difficult truth as he knew it.

In the past fifteen years or so, she and Santos would see each other only around Christmastime when they could afford to spare the time and the plane fare, and that amounted to about every other year, she explained. There wasn't much family business ever to attend, because the two women had been the only incumbents. Tina's father had been gone since she was a little girl and both her parents were gone by her twentieth birthday. Among their would-be cousins and other quazi-in-laws walking the sod, they only kept in touch with each other, which by their measure, was the sum of official family affairs.

The detective asked how frequently she had talked with Santos by phone. She said it wasn't a weekly thing but often monthly, and reiterated that they'd always been close. He asked what she might have heard Santos say about new friends or lovers, old flames, jilted characters, other suspects, or any change in habits or lifestyle. No, no, no, she said nothing she could think of, and that anyway Tina was a modern woman and had always done well at taking care of herself. He asked if Santos ever mentioned professor Skip Foster or his associate Daisy Wilson. Yes of

course, the art professor and the cook, she
said.

"She introduced me to them two winters
ago. We all went to a dinner theater
together," she said. "We missed last year, so
that trip was the last time I saw her. She
was planning to fly out here this year, I
booked her tickets last month, and that was
the last time we talked."

The detective explained, he didn't have
any preponderant suspects but Foster and
Wilson were parties of interest sincee they
were the only people significantly involved
with Tina recently, in any romantic sense.

"As far as I can tell," he said. It was a
mostly true statement.

"Well, if you have to ask, so they say," she remarked.

"And I have to look closely at all such relationships, under the circumstances. Victims of violent crime are typically not strangers to their attackers and they are statistically likely to be romantically involved with them."

"Oh?" she said.

He had elected not to mention R. Thompson's recent interaction with Santos for several reasons not the least of which being that he did not suspect him, although Thompson did, procedurally, so qualify.

He told her the body was still at the Pierce County Coroner's Office, and relayed

Wilson's offer to cover memorial and estate arrangements. He did not mention sharks or werewolves or any of the other rich mixture that had been hitting so close to home in Tacoma. They did discuss the unavoidable complexities of the matter pursuant to Santos' status as a performing artist.

Change of Venue

Returning non-stop to Washington state he slept through most of the flight. Two-forty-five Thursday morning, back at Sea-Tac the terminal contained a smattering of rained-on, half-asleep people. He walked to his vehicle and drove home to meet the early day. He did laundry, cleaned house, and mulled Foster's and Wilson's whereabouts last Friday and Saturday night. When he got to the office about seven, lieutenant MacKinney was already there. Coroner Dixie Thompson rang his desk about eight:

"Tina Santos' next of kin just called, I believe you are acquainted with Ms. Allison," she said. "She said her cousin's remains will not travel east, the services are here instead. It looks like the game is coming to you."

"Did she say why?" he asked.

"I didn't ask. She volunteered the

information to me. The service is Saturday," she said.

Around nine, MacKinney took a briefing from Smith:

"I'm catching up with OPD's David Wallace today. The victim in his case was a 29-year-old musician named Katherine Wells, whose band regularly played the venues in Olympia's old downtown. About eleven-thirty Saturday night she left on foot from her last gig. A few blocks away at the Port of Olympia Marine Terminal, Monday morning, longshoremen found what little was left of her chopped to bits," Smith explained. "That's all detective Wallace had for me last time I saw him. Hopefully his story's longer today."

"What else?" MacKinney asked. The man was task oriented, not impatient.

"A fine arts professor and his cohabitant chef girlfriend. Picture-perfect post-modern birds of Santos' feather and they all pay rent at Kelly Sammys pub," he cited. "It's tough to say how hot the love triangle was. I think it was long term though. Apparently they were the only romantic interest."

"Except Thompson," MacKinney clarified.

"Right."

"Do they have alibis?"

"Yes, generally."

"What about Philadelphia?"

"She'll be here for the funeral."

Denver Day

He phoned Wallace. Before pressing for vicarious progress, Smith reported the news of quazi-suspects Wilson and Foster sponsoring Santos' formalities. In Tacoma, no less. The information seemed to lighten Wallace's spirits which probably meant he had no new leads.

"So, Wells was the bass player in a straightedge punk metal group. No drugs, no alcohol, no smoking, none of it, and her community has already replaced her. They're driven, squared-away people, you know the type," Wallace said. "I talked to all the band members. None of them saw her leave. All of them live downtown, none of them own a car and the assumption is she left on foot. Or tried to. She didn't have a boyfriend because

she refused to date men, so this is also a
sexual assault investigation, and in that
respect different than the Santos case."

"Right. And Tina Santos suffered only one
axe wound," Smith said. "Do you see any
new links with Tacoma?"

"Not right out, but you know there must
be, incidental or not. Wells' was no jazz
quintet but it's the same industry and the
crimes were only thirty miles apart.
Connections are connections and a meaningful
one isn't a stretch," he said. Detective
Wallace told Smith he could feel free to
interview Wells' band himself, an attitude for
which Smith was grateful, considering the
proximity and sensitivity of both cases. Some
other detective might've gotten territorial and

thrown a tantrum.

"Those boys are pissed off," Wallace went on. "I believe they're at a loss for suspects but they'd really like to know, if you know what I mean."

"Maybe I should invite them to Saturday's funeral," Smith said.

Sea Dogs

Late morning, Smith drove himself back to the Foster-Wilson condo. Nobody was home. The next stop was Wilson's first shift, a restaurant that didn't open until dinner.

Wilson and two other prep cooks were already to hand, in and out of the back door with supplies in preparation of soup, bisque, and chowder; cutting vegetables, marinating prizes, and tinkering with sauces. He parked in front, walked around back, and waved at Wilson. She was carrying a stack of boxes from a storage shed to the kitchen's back door. She pointed him inside.

The back of the house was an orderly, clean, spacious, and well-equipped situation of stainless steel, gas burners, and wood-fired ovens, crowned with an array of hanging points and edges.

"Another woman has been killed with an

axe," he copped, "this time down in Oly."

"Same person?" she said.

"Maybe, always maybe, but the style is totally different. Tina was only hit once but this woman was pulped," Smith answered. "The correlation is tempting, notwithstanding other important differences."

He watched her eyes for embers of jealousy, conflict, surprise, arousal, deception, omission, and other faint taints. She stirred a pesto sauce and an undramatic minute passed before Smith continued.

"She played with a straightedge punk band and the Olympia police say the musicians are vengeful, frankly," he said. "All things being equal, by rights their disposition is justiciable in terms of natural law. I'll ask you this now, though: Where were you Friday and Saturday nights?"

"Kelly Sammys on Friday, Skip and me. We stayed home Saturday," she answered.

"Stayed in by yourselves?" Smith asked.

"Yes. By the way, Tina's aunt Janice will be here tomorrow afternoon," she said. "The memorial service is Saturday morning at eleven."

Smith realized it was a gamble to divulge information to Wilson, but he was out of leads and time was of the essence, so he set the bait.

Wells' band were gathered within fifteen

minutes of detective Smith's arrival at their home. Better said, the drummer showed up fifteen minutes after Smith got there to complete the scene where everybody else was already present, including their new bassist. They sat on the porch lunching on chips and hummus. The wood-frame house was an old rental bearing proud scars from generations of communal student dwelling.

He explained Wells' death might be the work of a serial killer, so their helping to court responsible parties to justice could prevent more killing.

"It is in everyone's best interest," he said, "to get to the bottom of this mess promptly." He made sure to mention the when and where of Santos' memorial service. They said they would be in touch.

About three that afternoon, detective Wallace phoned Smith's desk.

"Something weird has come up, but it will be well worth your trip. Meet me back at the port terminal in an hour." Wallace announced.

Smith finished his sandwich on the way to his car and, half hour later, arrived again at the Port of Olympia Marine Terminal. Wallace's unmarked police cruiser was already there.

He was greeted with a "you gotta see this." They walked toward the dock side, north and west of where Wells was found.

Denver Day

A great white shark hooked through the caudal fin hung upside down from a scale hook. The dock supervisor said it was a female, about fifteen-hundred pounds. There was an axe handle protruding from the fish's throat.

Ad hoc guesswork ensued regarding whether the axe was shoved into the animal's maw as a deliberate act, or if the shark was snacking on somebody who, incidentally, had an axe. Speculation persisted as to who might've hung the shark on that hook. Opinions varied, but all agreed it felt wrong to call it coincidence, even if the axe wasn't the murder weapon.

Russian Egg

While she was still on the hook, one of
the longshoremen opened the big fish with
an incision and the group beheld a sight, at
which no mariner or homicide detective
would blush for having flinched. At first it
looked like a large monkey in a kilt. But for
the mystery of an axe-wielding monkey in
the ocean the scenario was plausible enough
because great whites often take their meals
whole. The man who sliced open the shark
reached in with his arm and pried at the
object. It tumbled onto the deck. At their

feet lay the first shark-regurgitated werewolf anyone had ever seen.

All stared on. Wallace executed a sturdy one-liner and Smith voiced a few obvious facts. The men poked lightly at the darkly miraculous abomination.

"This may be an early warning sign that our work is done," Smith warned. "It puts upon us the same as what's undone the investigations of the October 11 killings."

"Yeah. Until now Olympia had avoided the monkey business," Wallace said, begrudgingly. "I will make a collegiate effort at thinking of this shark as innocent until proven guilty."

"Nobody has determined exactly how come

they're walking the good earth, but a couple of my associates can brief you about what they do know," Smith said. "I can have our coroner come down here tomorrow. She's seen some things."

It was around four by now. Detective Wallace telephoned Thurston County dispatch and asked for someone to come to the port with a heavy bag. En route I-5 north back to Tacoma, Smith phoned R. Thompson:

"Oly and Thurston County have another one of those things you've been chasing. They cut it out of the gut of a great white shark this morning, after dockworkers found it the fish hanging from a scale hook." he reported. "There was an axe stuck in her throat."

"The shark's throat or the furry's throat?" Thompson followed.

"The shark's," Smith answered. "If it makes any difference. Recall, the port terminal is where they found the Olympia woman last weekend. There are some important differences between the OPD case and ours; Their victim was raped, and hacked into chum. But now, this does present a demoralizing correlation between both axe killings and the creatures."

"What was she wearing?" Thompson asked.

"The victim?"

"No, the creature."

"Some kind of cheerleader uniform, you

can see for yourself in the morning," Smith answered. "That shark and the thing from its gut are in transport to the Thurston County Coroner's Office where we'll meet everybody in the morning. I told them Dixie would come too, are you willing?"

"You're welcome, I'll persuade Dixie," Thompson said. "I can tell you and OPD and Thurston County medical and whoever else is listening what I have seen. I can't explain it but I can speculate."

S. Smith was discouraged and coolly ambivalent about the new development. The matter begged a number of questions.

Probably the easiest of the various possibilities was the shark and its last supper were unrelated to the Santos and Wells cases, the downside of that interpretation being its net lack of particular development in the two homicide investigations, and its general implications about the ubiquity of werewolves.

The bright side of anachronistic, irrelevant werewolves? It wouldn't relegate his job to barking at the moon like what had mired Thompson and countless other agencies from here to Mexico, but Smith felt his luck along those lines was running out.

The axe in the shark and the repeat involvement of the unlucky marine terminal, by their own rights, were compelling if seemingly anomalous. Discounting its hopeful irrelevance, the axe in hand was hard evidence of something albeit unknown. But the creature cast a shadow of hopelessness since the contents of the shark's stomach pierced the veil between axe and werewolf. Any such correlation might easily illumine fatal flaws pursuant to proper adjudication of the Santos and Wells cases.

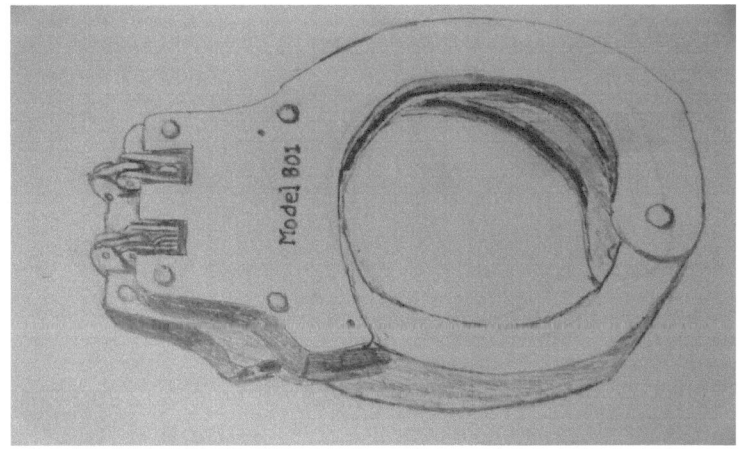

Alpha Taxonomy

Returning from Olympia, he went to the

coroner's office where Dixie was locking up for the day. He explained his newfound interest in the troubling contents of her body locker and she ogled him lengthwise.

"Yeah, I heard, you too," she declared. "Oh brother."

"Yes now me, and Oly P.D. too, among others. May I look at our collection?"

They walked back to the fridge.

"Collection is a fitting word. Also by the way, I am ready to authorize the release of Santos' body, if you are done with it," Dixie said. "Her people want her back so they can plant her."

She uncovered four werewolves and seven regular human victims killed during her ex-husband's Saturday night fight at Davey Jones Lickers HQ.

Coroner Thompson also showed him some of the prior week's local victims; the stripper and the pizza delivery guy killed at the Squeezebox nightclub on October 11.

A third October 11 victim's body had been stolen from the morgue, as had the stripper's. The stripper's corpse had turned up a second time as a dead post-op werewolf, alongside two of R. Thompson's main suspects, stripper Keri Anders and general puke Louis Ho.

An interesting piece of hopefully useless trivia is that Ho's and Anders' bodies were good examples of what werewolves can do in bed. Just nevermind, if you can. Anyway, Dixie pointed at the werewolves.

"As you see, two of them are headless courtesy of a twelve-gauge shotgun," she said. "Their hands and feet are tied, but none of them came back from the dead at this location. Not technically, anyway, because this girl's corpse was stolen before she re-animated. These returning surprises have been also happening elsewhere. Last week in Oakland, one of them sat up during its own autopsy and gobbled up an assistant coroner."

"Saturday, around the time of our most recent batch incoming here, many of the October 11 stripper bodies, from Eugene to southern California, denied their custodians, with mayhem ensuing at the nightclubs of their erstwhile employment. Anyway look at these uniforms, detective."

She pointed: "These particular ones were from the Chino Wheeled Beavers roller derby team who drowned last week inside their team ambulance in the San Francisco Bay. Later they disappeared like so many free donuts from the Alameda County Coroner's keep. It was one of those who had that deputy coroner's number, and it was their ambulance which we burned Monday, in our tow lot. That the ones who aren't here remain at large is good news to nobody."

Smith looked at the names on the jerseys of the four werewolves: Rolling Pinny. Lightning Pelt. Plasma Hat. The Milkmaid. He studied the room full of monsters and their victims for another quarter hour, and photographed them. Before departing Dixie's company, the detective took one last look at Santos and her head wound, and completed a form to authorize the release of her body from county custody.

In light of the security problems currently troubling coroners' offices, Pierce County was still staffing hers with shotgun-wielding deputies pursuant to advice from the FBI. Smith and D. Thompson nodded to that detail on their way out.

It occurred to the detective that Thursday evening is a pretty auspicious constellation for the university crowd, so he drove to Kelly Sammys. The place was thick with thinkers, and drinkers. The bartender he'd met earlier took his order for a guaca-bean burger and soda with bitters.

"Tina's funeral is Saturday," Smith mentioned.

"Yep. It is being billed as a wake that begins and ends right here. Should be a who's who of bar regulars," the barman said.

Foul Hook

Smith went home from Kelly Sammys for

a last night of sleep before his work became the stuff of nightmares. By eight Friday morning, he and Thompson, and Thompson's ex-wife, were southbound for the Thurston County Coroner's Office. Both detectives took their cars, "in case one of us gets eaten by a shark," detective Thompson said.

Dixie rode with Smith who thought detective Thompson looked like he'd been up all night. Wallace was waiting when they arrived and offered coffee. All politely declined except R. Thompson.

Coroner Thompson's Thurston County counterpart, Ben Jones, looked like he was in his early forties, with a curly, well-trimmed beard of burgundy and gray. He walked them back to the matters at hand, the wolf creature and shark, on separate tables.

"It's the first time I've ever worked with a shark," Jones said.

"Sharktopsy," Thompson said. His ex-wife snickered.

"The great white drowned in the dry air," Jones said. "The axe caused the fish's death only insofar as it was the lure which hooked her. But by who, and whose line?"

"We don't know. It had to be somebody," Wallace said. "Rough angling."

"But the mystery of the werewolf trumps the axe," Jones went on. "The thing was wearing a tube top, canvas high tops, and a black and pink bottom into the skirts of which is stitched the word 'Firepie'."

Jones pulled a ballpoint pen from his left pocket protector and pointed with it. They beheld Firepie Beaver.

"We know her," detective Thompson said, "so to speak. After the Alameda County search team fished her and her teammates and their team vehicle out of Saint Frankie Bay, she killed the last guy who tried to give her a forensic blade. These women were all drowned like wet rats in some old ambulance. Twenty of them. At first, she was the only one weird and hairy like this."

"Later," he continued, "the rest of the Chino Wheeled Beavers disappeared from the Alameda County morgue. Saturday night they came as werewolves, in their undead ambulance to the derby match in Tacoma, between the Davey Jones Lickers and the Seattle Plaiden Switches. They killed seven people, we killed four werewolves. All of those casualties are here. I don't know if Firepie was there Saturday, maybe she didn't arrive until this week, riding on a unicorn. But it's true, they do capriciously return from the dead and a stitch in time saves nine. So, tie her hands and feet. Now."

Jones nodded and ordered one of his staff to fetch a ligature. Dixie spoke next:

"We have five werewolf specimens at Pierce County; counting Ricky's four from Saturday night; the fifth was in plain, regular non-monster form when I processed her the first time," she said.

"Analysis of the werewolves showed a human physiology whose canine evolutionary traits somehow are hyper-accentuated. As if by some sort of instantaneous evolutionary retrograde. In other words, whatever is happening to them emphasizes, disproportionately, canine traits which are otherwise latent among the Homo sapiens sapiens."

"However, the chemical cocktail with which I embalmed our twice-dead client after her first post-mortem examination, when her body was still "normal," was absent from her system when she returned days later as a dead werewolf," Dixie said. "Which, I say, is a phenomena of metaphysics not genetics, but of course you could say the same thing about zombies, which, arguably, exactly what the werewolves are. Hairy ones."

"For round two, I did find a new cheeseburger in her craw, and my previous incision marks are still there, beneath the fur as are her tattoos. We think she transformed during sex," Dixie concluded.

"We have the, err, privilege of setting certain precedents with these werewolf investigations," detective Thompson added. "I suggest you burn both of those things, the shark and the werewolf, same as we did with that drowned ambulance in our tow lot. And, uh, Dixie, it's probably due time for us to incinerate our inventory of werewolves since they're less likely to return from ashes. We should have, in my opinion, put them in that ambulance before we torched it."

Denver Day

Jones and Wallace thanked the Thompsons for their input. D. Thompson and Jones exchanged some technical and scientific paperwork regarding various curiosities of the creatures. Wallace and Smith switched the subject over to Santos and Wells, and the group all took a viewing at Wells' unrecognizable, piecemeal, incomplete remains before adjournment.

"I talked to Wells' band and implicitly invited them to the wake Saturday," Smith said. "The Kelly Sammys bartender says the memorial will entail steady libations by his truly. Anything new?"

"Well, the world continues to spin on its own," answered Wallace, distracted, "and such revolution is a key to any investigation.

Meanwhile, I'd like to staff that Santos funeral if you don't mind. So, you really think we should burn this shark and this weird wolf-monkey thing?"

"You might. It's a valid, conservative option, which weighs of course against the destruction of rare, tangible, yet nonsensical evidence," Smith said. "But if you keep 'em, you better post a twenty-four hour watch."

Southbound Sock Hop

The erstwhile Thompsons rode together on the way back home, giving Smith more time, in his natural state of solitude, to consider recent developments.

Janice Allison would arrive later in the day for tomorrow's funeral, adding a dynamic to the Foster-Wilson duo which he hoped might make the couple more readable. Despite their weakening status as prime suspects, they were still parties of interest because of their significant involvement with the victim and their position to provide input about her world, and also because he was also feeding Wilson details about the case.

But they were clean, orderly, and probably innocent. Intellectuals. Busy professionals. Busy burying Santos, among other things. They had an elitist brown-leather kink; he had concluded their the odor was sex not violence, notwithstanding the similarity of the two which for some people are interchangeable. This was a homicide investigation, after all.

The detective remained uncertain about how much credence to give Olympia's shark and its disquieting stomach contents. Though the thing smacked of unimpeachable natural law of the sea, and, despite Thompson's investigation being a textbook study of why it's nearly impossible to peaceably and efficiently apprehend or logically prosecute actual supernatural entities, the axe in the big fish seemed like a clear and organized threat from someone or something, nevertheless.

Pursuant to due process and criminal

procedure, Smith was prepared to dismiss the
werewolf in the dead shark, as well as the
ones in Pierce County as unsolvable
nonsense. He felt sure any potentially
practical value they might have was exclusive
of objective relevance. Except that they were
accumulating and it was pretty much open
season on them, their forensic value was
poor. It seemed fine to consider them
philosophically criminal as natural
manifestations of evil but there was no
known secular protocol for their interdiction.
Thus, he made up his mind to ignore them.

Unexplainable? Probably. Logical? Go
werewolves. Dangerous? A fair assumption.

To him an axe, and a common shark,
were more accessible. Unlike mythological

creatures, the proper origin of the hardware was traceable, and that could lead to a normal, warm-blooded suspect.

Or not. At the end of the day it was just one wet axe in an extremely tenuous context. Quietly, Smith harbored a hunch that it was Santos' axe and probably the one used to kill both women. And why not? The fact was, Santos' old ranger's tool, thought to have been the murder weapon, had been missing from the crime scene.

Smith took a trip that afternoon to the hotel where Santos' band was the regular lounge act. He met with the back-of-the-house manager whose duties, he learned, included bar management, and the show booking and compensation of the live acts.

Denver Day

Once before he had met with this guy, who'd told him the band was still playing regularly and that there was still significant, regular foot traffic from the nearby Diddler On The Roof nightclub, along with a heavy flow of life insurance, encyclopedia, and vacuum cleaner salespeople (primarily males) coming in off the interstate. However, he gave no new insight regarding who were and who weren't axe murderers.

Again, Smith conveniently advertised Santos' funeral involving Kelly Sammys pub.

"You must be shorthanded if you're soliciting volunteer work from punk bands and bar managers," the man said.

"It takes a village."

Sitting in his boxer shorts that night about ten, watching sports news, the detective took a call from lieutenant MacKinney who bore bloody news. "Thompson is cleaning up an awful mess at a filling station on state highway 512 at I-5. He wants you down there now."

"On my way. Got any teasers?"

"More sharks I think. Good luck."

In order to contain the blood and guts, the staff on scene had already taped off and locked down the gas station. Smith arrived around ten-thirty. Thompson briefed him:

"There are no witnesses, as far as I can tell," he said. "The clerk's dead. Nobody, well no other human bodies, were found. Whoever called it in to city dispatch might've seen something but they didn't hang around and I don't blame them."

Indeed, there were flotsam and jetsam at the corner store. Pierce County deputies were putting the headless clerk on a stretcher as the two detectives stepped over the yellow tape and through the store's glass front door. The clerk's head had been bitten off by a shark, of which several were scattered anachronistically about a floor slick with displaced biology. One shark had taken several buckshot loads, probably the work of the attendant clerk. Another shark, maybe in retaliation for the shotgunning, had bitten off the clerk's head.

"How in the hell do these things go

about out of water?" Smith mused.

"I don't know, but they do," Thompson grumbled. "Here are the two other sharks, both of them beaten nearly flat with a baseball bat, apparently by this werewolf here."

He pointed, and there, hanging halfway out of one of the dead sharks (not the buckshot-filled one) was the carcass of a ballbat-wielding werewolf. She was one of the Chino Beaver morphs who had survived the local fight Saturday night.

"Get these sharks packed up too," Smith told county personnel, who had tags and bags. "Dixie can cut them open to see what other snacks they've had."

Greener Pastures

The Pierce County men bagged up the
three dead sharks, and decided to leave the
half-swallowed werewolf in the shark maw so
the evidence would be more pristine for Dixie
Thompson. All the new stiffies, including the
headless store clerk, were transported to the
morgue.

Unless any more monster fights or other
bizarro flare-ups happened before morning,
Smith thought it seemed less important to be

anywhere for now except the coroner's office to enjoy more sharktopsies.

"Smith, I have a date," R. Thompson announced, calling it a day after the bodies were hauled away. "You can stay up late with this lot if you want. I understand these sharks are right up your alley. Please tell Dixie I'll be there first thing in the morning to look again."

So, deputies mopped up the wet pink lacquer of multi-species goo while Smith and two of the city units made their way to the coroner's office. He and Dixie stayed and took photographs until around two.

The late clerk, a decomposing Chinese guy, had a Washington state driver license which defined him as Laurence Xjiang, age forty-eight. The circumstances of his terminal predicament were clearer after Dixie cut open the first shark, whose belly contained Xjiang's head, eyeglasses, and Seattle Mariners ballcap, a couple of sea bass, and a few bags of jalapeño flavored potato chips.

When Dixie opened the second big fish, the one peppered with buckshot, she discovered the corporal remains of Beep Beep Beaver of the Chino, California Wheeled Beavers derby team. Beep Beep, like Firepie Beaver, was another veteran of Saturday night's massacre fiasco in the Lickers parking lot. Tonight, however, she was no survivor. Not yet. Bit it was at least her second time to die, having first drowned in the San

Francisco Bay.

Shark number two had also eaten its fair share of regular seafood, as well as convenience store snacks, and the third sharktopsy revealed the top half of the werewolf who'd been partially swallowed head first and whose legs were still hanging out of the shark mouth. Stitched across the back of her derby skirt was her handle, Sugar. Sugar Beaver, indeed.

Someone made a joke. Sheriff's deputies and Smith helped Dixie remove the bottom-half-of wolfthing from the shark's throat using a long knife, a wooden rod, and some vegetable oil. Dixie placed the two werewolves on separate tables, then tied their hands and feet firmly.

Denver Day

Kelly Sammys was already at a rolling boil by its regular opening time of eleven Saturday, grandly fueled by Tina Santos' friends and loved ones and the many opportunistically or incidentally festive students and barflies whirling into the wide fetch of the saxophonist's wake. When Smith arrived, he noted the very dry, alert, and watchful members of Wells' straightedge punk band gathered, boozeless, in a booth; They countenanced their pride effectively by various states of plaid, standard colors, pressed t-shirts, felt, and slick heads. The detective nodded at them and they all nodded back.

Also, near the crowded bar was a booth full of Santos' band, playing cards solemnly and drinking black beer. The usual cat was behind the bar pouring pitchers and taking short-order tickets for the kitchen. The smell of the tavern this morning was a pedigree of coffee, porter, onion soup, and rain. Smith didn't see Foster and Wilson or Janice Allison anywhere yet.

The bar was mostly cleared at noon when the crowd went out into the weather and boarded a bus. Smith followed in his own vehicle. Likewise did various others, such as Wells' musician friends.

The plan was for the ceremony to be short, thirty minutes tops, then everyone would go back to the pub. As he pulled up to the graveyard, the detective took a call from the lieutenant: "How's the funeral?"

Denver Day

"There are lots of musicians and lots of drinking," Smith answered.

"Have fun. Say, I just took another call from Thompson. He's at the coroner's office, checking on the new monsters," MacKinney said. "So, he says his two new werewolves are still there but your three sharks are gone. Keep your eyes peeled, eh, and catch up with Dixie when you have time."

Smith hung up his phone, got out of the car, and walked towards the crowd. Foster, Wilson, and Allison were arrived and the ceremony just under way. In plainclothes a man and a woman began performing rites.

Nice Day For Hanging Around In Bars

The toddy of choice for Santos' boneyard ceremony was stout ale in Kelly Sammys draught glasses toted from tavern to bus to cemetery. Brief as the affair was intended to be brief, and provided with adequate weather conditions, the pints might have lasted through the entire presentation if nursed conservatively. Rain fell in the beverages and their custodians, and that was the best of it.

The couple performing the ceremony had the urn full of Santos' particulate remains.

Denver Day

The man unscrewed the lid and began sprinkling ash into the wet wind.

"OM AH HUM...In the palace of the Beatific Body wheel in the center of my physical throat, in the vast sphere immersed in rainbows and lights, in the center of the beatific wheel lotus, there is the clear, red, Evolutionary Great Scientist, Padmanarteshvara, with five light-ray brilliance, bliss-void united with the red Wisdom Angel, manifesting in space, holding chopper and skull bowl. May the body Scientist host protect all beings!"

Glowing and smiling brightly in the rain, the couple chanted the words together and detective Smith recognized the verse. They were quoting from *The Great Book of*

Natural Liberation Through Understanding the Between, a classic Buddhist text composed by Padma Sambhava.

Santos' wet hippie friends, musician friends, and barfly friends continued variously smoking and drinking unfazed. Despite the somber circumstances and weather a fairly jovial and sunny crowd was in place smiling and chatting. Wells' people had made fast friends with Santos', and they were talking shop. Several of them weren't even watching the ceremony. After all, it was a wake not meant to be morose, moreover, there were no inconsolable family members wailing tears of grief because Tina had next to zero family literally, and her friends and lovers were all artistic, philosophical, business-minded people.

Denver Day

R. Thompson arrived, also smoking, but instead of ale he was drinking coffee from the coroner's office pot. Exceptionally, Santos' next-of-and-only kin Janice Allison was already extremely drunk and so were Skip Foster and Daisy Wilson. The three of them were making out and were noisy, handsy, and horny with their game of grab-ass but nobody seemed to care.

It was in this relaxed atmosphere of festive memorial to the departed and among the somewhat divided attention of the crowd that an event occurred which could be considered relatively minor in light of the overall scheme of things in contemporary Tacoma. The occurrence caused a period of suspended awareness about the sequence of events, although Smith was pretty sure he saw what actually started it:

Some woman, who had been standing near the couple handling the bowlful of Santos' dusty remains, slipped in a muddy spot and fell into the urn-bearing woman who, putting the balance of the container before her own, quickly shoved it into the grasp of the other ceremonial partner. Her act of inter-dimensional altruism, however, failed and all three of them fell. Both women hit the ground first, then upon them landed the man.

And before he hit the ground, he'd tossed the urn. It was a last-ditch attempt because, knowing what he knew, he knew it would spill if he fell with it. But just as the lid would come off if a man fell with it, it would also come off when airborne.

Incidental to the man and the two women hitting the mud, and the contents of the urn puffing out into a short-lived ash plume above the crowd, there came an uncannily well-timed flash of lightning nearby along with a jolting a thunder clap. A drop in pressure brought the precipitation from steady to heavy immediately. Things remained below the threshold of mayhem, but just barely.

Thompson looked at Smith. They both instinctively backed a few more steps away from the entropy before them. The three fallen were helped up from the mud and a few more words were said for a proper but hasty closure of the ceremony. Then came sideways rain. Sheepishly but without delay, the people re-boarded the bus. The detectives chatted from driver-side window to driver-side window before leaving the cemetery.

"I hear the sharks are gone," Smith said.

"You heard right. She found little shark-shaped piles of sand where their carcasses were stored. I don't know whether they reanimated and hopped out or rolled out or what. Maybe they were stolen. They could have disintegrated like dead, murderous, evil, people-eating land fish might conceivably do," Thompson answered. "Get used to it, Smith. A trip to the morgue doesn't mean what it used to. And it's a Saturday again, word to the wise, be on your toes," he winked.

Denver Day

At Kelly Sammys, happy hour recom-
menced and carried into the afternoon.
Eventually, Allison, Foster, and Wilson
returned from an excursion to Foster and
Wilson's condo. They were all still drunk but
significantly steadier on their feet after post-
funeral sex. In comparison to what happened
a few minutes after their re-arrival at the
pub, the spontaneous urn dropping in the
cemetery looked like a tea party on starched
doilies for freshly perfumed kittens.

Sturdily bolted to the rafters above the
egress to the pub's restrooms was mounted a
large swordfish which somehow escaped its
moorings and fell head-and-pointy-nose-first
into an unsuspecting patron walking
underneath it, en route to the ladies' room.

110

Janice Allison. Was.

The fish's blade shoved itself truly and deeply into Allison's petite lower neck just above the very top of her sternum.

It was a racket loud enough that everyone in the noisy tavern caught it, but the shrieking didn't last long. The stuffed fish pierced her clavicle, heart, and intestinal cavity. It exited her body through the fleshy area about the anus. In well under a minute, Allison's blood had left the body, arcing from entrance and exit wounds. The late Tina Santos' aunt Jan died quickly on the beery hardwood floor of Kelly Sammys.

Custom Of The Sea

Janice Allison was still threaded onto the swordfish when the sheriff's office took her away. It would've made an even bigger mess of the tavern floor if they tried to unhook her there, anyway.

As the revelers were sheepish in resuming their bender after its subject's ashes were fumbled in the muddy cemetery, they were outright bashful with the libations beyond the gruesome demise of Santos' aunt. The music barely stopped, though.

The storm continued all day. At dusk it went from buckets to barrels. Winter in the American Northwest arrived with a low pressure system parked above the region for the weekend if not the month. Temperatures dropped. There was an offshore gale warning.

Dixie was checking out the newest abomination in her metastasizing collection of inanimate oddities. She took a call from Thurston County Coroner Jones regarding the confounding disappearance of the gutted great white shark in whose belly Firepie Beaver was discovered. But they still had (what was left of) Firepie, he said; in fact, as he hadn't taken steps to chemically preserve the werewolf's corpse, Jones reported it had (rather than rising from the dead) actually begun decomposing properly. So far, so good.

Beyond spilling Santos like so much bongwater in the mud at her own funeral, and the ensuing kebabization of her auntie, and, the land-going sharks' disappearance from the Thurston and Pierce county morgues, nothing else too wacky had occurred that day, despite detective Thompson's wry and recurring warnings to Smith. Nevertheless, caveats from R. Thompson were valuable and honest guidelines disregarded only by fools.

The rest of the night was OK in town. Tacoma's own Davey Jones Lickers were on the road and won the evening's match, on the week's anniversary of the extremely fatal tailgate party in their warehouse parking lot.

Instead of sunlight, in due course the dawn brought a wintry mix. Lieutenant MacKinney's home phone rang during breakfast Sunday with a call from the investigative unit of the U.S. Coast Guard's Seattle Sector, who said they wanted to talk with the Washington State Police employee who was in charge of shark or doglady related killings.

The man didn't elaborate during the conversation although his message was plain, to wit, the recent zombie business was no longer a matter landlocked. The lieutenant gave him Thompson's contact information.

Denver Day

Thompson interrupted Smith's Sunday hibernation so the two of them could meet with the Coast Guard investigator for lunch at the diner. The three of men ordered various specials with iced tea. The coastie's story was well suited for the dark weather.

"About two this morning, a commercial fishing boat in the sound contacted us. They couldn't raise their friends on a little twin diesel called the *Blint Mary*," the officer said. "The captain said their last radio communication was about midnight and he estimated the ship was somewhere near the mouth of the sound when they lost contact. There was no EPIRB or other distress-type signal. About an hour after we took that call, one of our patrols painted a boat drifting thirty miles west of Ozette. That turned out to be the *Blint Mary,* crewless. We towed it down to Westport. No words can do justice, but I will show you."

Continuous little clear rivers of cold rain flowed down the diner's glass window.

"Did you find some werewolves on that boat, commander?" Thompson asked.

"Yeah," he answered, "along with remnants of the crew and some sharks. So, I heard you guys were working on this stuff."

They finished their lunches, got back out into the weather, and followed their new friend in Thompson's sedan. It was a rainy, hilly drive that took around two hours.

"Some funeral yesterday," Smith said.

"A stuffed swordfish in the neck and out the southern can," Thompson said. "Ouch."

"Our shark-spects from Friday night have disintegrated in the morgue," Smith mulled, "the Olympia shark disappeared too."

"Welcome to the rest of your life," Thompson said. "I wonder if they talk. What if we could, you know, catch one alive?"

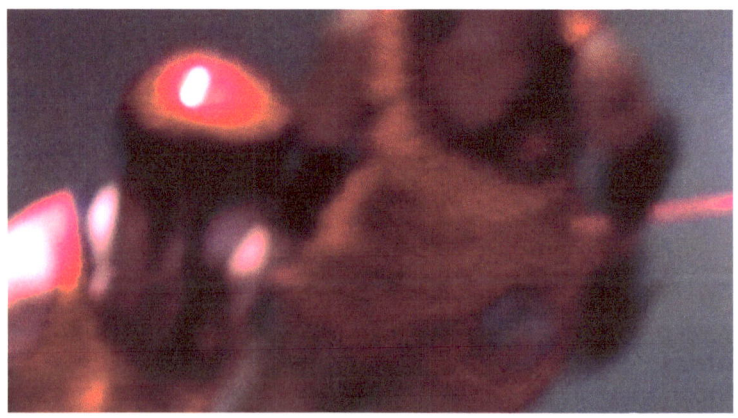

Opening Day

Rain persisted as Smith, Thompson, and

the Coast Guard officer made their way to the last dock of Westport's northernmost pier, where at a distance, the *Blint Mary* looked quaint, weathered, and willing. At closer inspection the vessel was exactly as the search crew found it that morning, the bodies inside remained undisturbed. The rain had washed away most of the blood on deck, but there remained scads of evidence of something gone terribly wrong.

"She had a crew of eight. We found one of them intact, the captain. Below deck," the officer said, pointing down. "We found half a man on the bridge, and we found two of those hairy things, one below deck and the other on the bridge. And some sharks; and that's what gets me. In very many real ways

Denver Day

I've seen my share of wolf ladies in my day, as it were. But never sharks topside without a line. Time was but time ain't no more."

They inspected the deck before climbing up to the bridge. There was scattered gear and tackle, and fresh bullet holes in the cabin walls. Seamens arms and hooks had been scrambled to answer the rabid teeth and razor-sharp claws a guerrilla assault.

In the cabin they observed: (1) most of one of the crewman whose head and upper torso were removed by a shark, evidently; (2) two dead sharks; and (3) a dead werewolf. It was hard to tell who killed whom but for obvious logical eliminations, i.e. the crewmen probably hadn't bitten any of his mates in half and sharks aren't nimble with shotguns.

Within the cabin, the walls were spattered with buckshot holes. The other shark had been sliced in half with a blade or, maybe a rigged line. Notably, the werewolf wore the red kilt of a Phoenix Bloody Roller, not the black and pink of Chino's Wheeled Beavers. Another Bloody Roller, perforated with stab wounds, was still entangled with the captain's rigorous body.

"All I know to say is, the boat was boarded by fish and animals, close-quarters fisticuffs followed, and here we stand," the officer said. "And except for the remains of the two, the rest of the crew's missing."

"Well, that's all that anyone can say," Thompson said.

Smith mentioned the recent shark-and-werewolf-related event at the Oly Marine Terminal, and the skirmish among the landgoing Carcharodon carchariases and anatomically modern Canis lupus lupuses at the convenience store in Tacoma.

"The wolf lady thing has been going on a couple of weeks longer than the shark thing," Thompson said. "Anyway, we've declared open hunting season on all of them."

"It's futile and naïve to keep at this problem with our peaceable criminal procedure and monocles," Smith said. "But hunting air sharks and marine werewomen has its challenges."

Nonplussed, the officer was smiling the

smile of a stoic mariner who's seen his fair share of seaborne weirdness. "For sure we will do what we can, keeping sharp ears and eyes for you," he said. "Want the bodies?"

"No. Thank you. We have plenty. Those belong to the people of the United States of America," Thompson said. "Watch the werewolves because they have a tendency to reanimate, keep their limbs bound, or better yet, burn 'em. Meanwhile the sharks are prone to entirely disappear or disintegrate. They all make excellent firewood."

It was pushing nine when the two dicks got back to Tacoma. They stopped at Kelly Sammys for mashed potatoes and soup. Except the missing swordfish, the shanty had no new scars. The usual barman shrugged at them, as if to acquit himself. After dinner, Thompson dropped Smith off at the station.

"I'm going to watch T.V. in my underwear, we can discuss hunting season tomorrow," Thompson said. Smith went back to the morgue.

Tack

Dixie placed the shark sand into glass jars. The labels read:

"SHARK SAND NO. 1 (ate Laurence Xjiang)"

"SHARK SAND NO. 2 (ate Beep Beep Beaver)"

"SHARK SAND NO. 3 (ate Sugar Beaver)"

Smith considered these items in the fluorescent light of the coroner's laboratory. He could see a few pellets of buckshot in one of the sand samples. Beep Beep and Sugar were still bound, tabled, and for now, still dead. And still fresh-looking. D. Thompson had pumped them full of coroner's cocktails despite the various documented instances of post-embalming reanimation.

The four werewolves and the seven regular humanoids killed Saturday-before-last in the parking lot massacre were still there. Some of the local victims from the original October 11 nightclub killings, along with a number of the original best suspects thereof, remained as well in Pierce County custody.

Meanwhile, Janice Allison and the swordfish stayed fused. Dixie had troubled to put that macabre hybrid on ice but she'd put off disentanglement until Monday morning.

He mused about how to catch a live werewolf. Typically they didn't show up at the morgue until they were already dead. Yes, somebody had burgled this very morgue recently, and yes, the identity of the perpetrators wasn't apparent by way of the surveillance tape, but no, the burglars weren't thought to have been werewolves.

Although there had been some skirmishes among various undead derby teams, the real bile right now seemed the most corpulent between the derby wolves and the ambulatory sharks. Still, regular people were being caught in the crossfire of the feud.

Maybe the sharks could be formidable bait for catching a live werewolf? Would sprinkling shark dust about some likely location make do for a werewolf trap? Is a werewolf carcass effective shark bait?

No conjecture was made for how catching anything alive might actually help. It was an investigative fishing expedition as everyone was running out of ideas, and a logical way forward under circumstances in which logic, otherwise, was bankrupt.

Denver Day

Suddenly aware of his compounded fatigue, Smith locked the door behind him with a shudder and went home to a dreamless sleep. The rain persisted into Monday and by eight, Smith, Thompson, and MacKinney were sitting around the coffee pot discussing shark fishing with wolf carcasses, and what or who might be sprinkled with shark dust to attract live ones.

"I think we need a boat. And tackle, we could bring a few werewolves for bait but not all of them," the lieutenant said. "Potentially, I mean hopefully they're a finite resource, you know."

Thompson smirked at their supervisor's animated interest in the new and exciting opportunities at supernatural sportsmanship.

"I'll ask the Coast Guard command if they are interested in helping," McKinney said.

"OK. And later this week we'll set out shark bait around town and lay in the wait," Thompson said. "Maybe the Davey Jones Lickers will chip in with the effort too, they seem to be gung ho."

Too Quiet

Some weeks before the West Coast's October 11 stripper murders, one of the

Denver Day

Phoenix Bloody Rollers was killed in a bench-clearing brawl at a San Diego roadhouse; Some of the victim's teammates and roommates had been interviewed in the wake of October 11. Detective Joe Lopez of the San Diego city force had flown to Phoenix to meet some of the surviving Bloody Rollers. After wolfladies began popping up in Western cities, there was a Schrödinger's-catlike incident whereby the Flagstaff derby team apparently went missing on their way home from a match with the Bloody Rollers, and, Maricopa County authorities reported the active Bloody Rollers were also gone without a trace after that match.

In conflict with those missing-persons

reports, various sports fans in Arizona nevertheless reported neither the Phoenix nor the Flagstaff teams showed up for that derby match in the first place. But when numerous other fans were interviewed by police, they recalled watching the derby in its entirety, and talking with various of the players, et cetera. It was seemed a bifurcation of reality.

Because San Diego was where the roller derby weirdness began, Smith and Thompson knew Lopez could have valuable anecdotal information from that initial investigation of the inter-regional derby circuit. And since the cat was dragging, as it were, undead Bloody Rollers way up into the Pacific Northwest, R. Thompson telephoned Lopez in San Diego, trying to get some notion of the Phoenix

Denver Day

Bloody Rollers census beyond those already accounted for as dead werewolves. The investigators-come-sporting-gentlemen wanted to better understand the history, origins, and battle standards of their quarry.

Meanwhile the Monday morning breakroom table talk kept up among MacKinney, Thompson, and Smith, of how they might proceed with their brave yet half-baked plans for hunting.

"What's the difference, between regular sharks, and ones that knock over convenience stores and box on boat decks?" Smith said. "The sharks we're looking for should be hunted on land, else we're literally fishing."

"Such is guesswork. Anyway, the main

thing we're looking for offshore is werewolves not sharks," Thompson said.

Smith stayed skeptical but optimistic. "Using dead werewolves as bait on land might be effective," he said. "We could load up a truckload of 'em and head for the next Lickers match."

"We agree that the Lickers' warehouse on game night is a prime opportunity," Thompson said, and continued his hardsell for a seaborne expedition. "A good ship on standby is important, but the *Blint Mary*, specifically, she is touched. We might have the most success trolling for offshore werewolves in that particular boat, and there'd be no need to bait a line. We'll fish for monsters using their own freaky kharma as bait. MacKinney is negotiating that boat for us."

"Fine," Smith capitulated, "but you let your Davey Jones Lickers know, we will be at their next match with bells on."

Fifteen minutes later, MacKinney announced that Coast Guard brass was optimistic, and confirmation was pending for allocation of a crew and access to the *Blint Mary,* for the purpose of interagency collaboration for official state police business.

Ears In The Water, Eyes In The Hills

During lunch, Thompson took a return call from detective Lopez of the San Diego PD.

"Basically, I can't get in touch with the two roommates, of the Phoenix Bloody Rollers derby, whom I flew out to interview in

Denver Day

Arizona," Lopez said. "The names are Becca
and Veronica Roller. It's been more than a
week since I talked to them, which was
before the various, and conflicting, reports of
their disappearance. Anyway, the official
consensus among the authorities in Maricopa
County is, both teams' full rosters are
missing without a trace."

"Well," Thompson said. "I guess that
sheds some light on my situation, if only in
a rather tenuous, left-handed way. Right now
we're trying to defend ourselves from these
werewolves, hatching plans to hunt them
down, and now encountering reinforcements
in Bloody Rollers uniforms. What I'm trying
to say is, we've encountered some Bloody
Rollers in werewolf form and we make the

136

conservative assumption that they're all up here now."

"I'm happy to help you but I can't get official clearance for it," Lopez said. "Not without special funding. There's no slush fund here for apocalyptic junkets."

"Call it a vacation. I promise it's worth your time," Thompson suggested. "Did I mention maniac out-of-water sharks have entered the fray? And the werewolves have taken to maritime operations. Tomorrow we're trawling for them, with help from the U.S. Coast Guard."

After lunch, Thompson briefed the office regarding the latest news from Arizona. Meanwhile, the use of the *Blint Mary* staffed with a Coast Guard crew had been confirmed for their initial outing.

"Get out on the water. Keep your heads down," the lieutenant said. "Take a couple of days. Enjoy yourselves. And I'm working on new funding for the interdiction of "unprecedented phenomena," you know, werewolves and zombies and such. The name of the game is inter-agency cooperation, people. So go sell it."

Thompson and Smith returned to their respective bachelor pads, packed their gear, hit the rack, and slept like logs. First thing next morning they headed back to Westport, arriving after a ninety-minute drive to meet the interim crew of the *Blint Mary*.

They suited up with wool-insulated rain gear, and boarded. The bodies had been removed since their last visit and the gory blemishes were fewer, but there were still plenty of reminders from Sunday morning's horror. The vessel shoved off on a northerly course making way toward the area of the previous crew's last radio transmission.

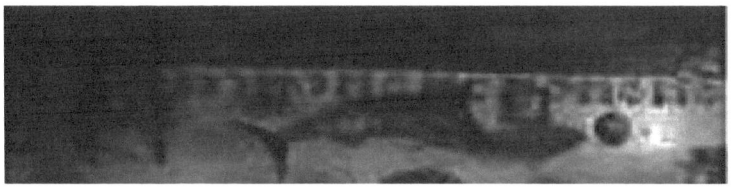

Scooby Don't

The first thing Dixie did when she got to work Monday was gaze in awe at the disturbing final embrace of Janice Allison. Because Allison was from out of state, in attendance of a memorial for her only known next of kin, it was possible no one would claim her body. With that, D. Thompson considered the wisdom of leaving the macabre situation entirely intact as it was, since she might get the chance to simply shove it all into the incinerator. Also, she didn't want to disturb evidence, however the facts of the woman's demise were just gory, not nuanced. So in a collegiate effort to cut bait she separated Allison's body from the stuffed fish.

Rick Thompson and Scott Smith had visited her on their way out of town, to obtain samples of the shark dust. Probably, they would also be using some of the creatures' corpses for monster baiting later in the week, they said. What could go wrong? Dixie was starting not to give a damn about those things anymore either, but she fully expected to see more of them.

In their rain gear, the detectives and two crewmen stood on the deck, watching the coastline pass by in the distance as the *Blint Mary* made her way north to the estimated location of Sunday's attack. They discussed the wisdom of diving the area in order to see what or who might be down there; the bottom was relatively shallow because they were still on the continental shelf. Smith had a funny feeling and he was not sure whether it was seasickness, skepticism, or something worse.

"No problem. We'll dive it tomorrow," one of the crewman said, a man named Aarons who looked to be in his early twenties. The

crew monitored nearby traffic. There were
some commercial vessels in the area, a
tanker loaded with black gold making way
south, and a number of fishing vessels
farther out. The navigator advised of an
unidentified, unlit vessel a couple miles
behind.

"Keep an eye on her, and be vigilant,"
the captain instructed, "don't hail or
approach. Let's just observe from afar. Even
if it is them, and it's probably not, I doubt
they'll try anything. They won't have any
luck boarding us."

He killed the diesels. Thompson lit a
cigarette. They floated to the sound drizzle
and mild chop.

That afternoon, detective Lopez and the SFPD sergeant of detectives Sam Carrasco, discussed the potential value of Lopez vacationing in the Great Northwest. "I can't resist the opportunity to see one, much less an opportunity to arrest one. They're trying to get funding, but I'm willing to take vacation time if I have to."

"For the time being, it'll have to be vacation, but you have my personal approval and I'll pitch-in with travel expenses," Carrasco said. "Enjoy yourself, make it a long weekend."

Of course nobody yet, not Lopez, not R. Thompson, not the Oakland PD, nor anybody else had been able to close any of the October 11 homicide cases, or any of the ones from the killings of a week later that had happened after the respective morgues were cleared without explanation.

Purgatory, Lopez thought, and he was probably right. That was part of the reason he decided to go hunting up north. It was a situation where everybody was failing to serve and protect from werewolves dining on West Coast nightlife and making a random but increasingly widespread buffet of the at-large citizenry.

Your Girlfriend Is A Dog?

"Lopez, there are two very attractive women here to see you," Carrasco said, craning his head over the side of his cubicle. "Said their names are Becca and Veronica."

Lopez motioned in the affirmative, and a minute later a clerk from the front of the house escorted the two women to his space. Becomingly, they spoke first.

"We read it on the winds you're headed

north to fight werewolves in the name of natural man-sport and universal moral obligation," Becca Roller started, smiling at him. In his previous dealings with these girls, Veronica Roller had done most of the talking. He looked at the tawny, bright eyed, thick skinned, heavily tattooed women. Their hair had changed color since he'd last seen them.

"We can help you find, catch, and kill them," she continued.

"OK," Lopez said. "But, are you aware, that you guys, both the Rollers and the Flagstaff derby team, are officially classified as missing persons?"

"Well, yes, that would follow," Becca said.

146

"The present uncertainty of our civil status is one of the results of our knowledge about the werewolves. Look at me, Joe."

He looked at her, she met his eyes. She smiled and made a rapid licking motion with her tongue, a blurry flickering like a snake's. Becca's face flushed and her hair swirled as it lit up like fiberoptic wire spewing every imaginable color. She was pulsing. Lopez was entirely affixed.

He stared into her binocular gaze, somehow physically trapped. The woman's eyes glowed an ember-orange plasma, flashed bright green then pulsed high blue. Lopez could not move his muscles, nor avert or close his eyes, nor squirm, nor even breathe. Then Veronica lit up also, glowing in his

147

peripheral vision and he felt the room's
energy double.

After some unknown amount of time, he
could move again, as both women simmered
back to their normal ruddy ambiance, smiling
warmly at officer Lopez.

"Don't worry buddy. We're the good ones."

The electromagnetic charge in the room
remained pretty high. Joe Lopez' hair stood
on end and he was still physically thrilled.
Then they placed their warm hands directly
on him and smiled at his insides. It was
obvious to him, they were telling the truth
about their benevolence. He felt it, that their
energy was good. What earlier he couldn't
understand about them, he now knew.

Having shown themselves, even though they were "back to normal," he still could see their subtle glowing beyond the threshold of visual perception. It was unmistakable, now that he knew what to look, or feel, for. Theirs was like a shiny coat; part fur, part light.

"Furthermore, detective Lopez, we are somewhat numerous. Most of both the Flagstaff team, and our own Roller teammates, are of the same nature as us," Veronica said, finally speaking up. "On the other hand, the base, murderous, hairy things which your peers have encountered cannot talk, do not glow, and are essentially just violent, murderous, hungry ghosts with sharp teeth and mangy fur. They're prone to killing, and travel quickly and stealthily. They're empty but fast and mean. Be careful."

Becca added: "As far as we can sense, the base and filthy ones are only loose at the western extremities of this continent. So far. They're hiding in and around the cities where they've already made attacks. Also, we know all of the Chino girls went to the dark side, but they may have doubles like us, and some of your Davey Jones Lickers are with us too."

"Washington State Police Detective Thompson says the Coast Guard found two dead Bloody Rollers at sea," Lopez said.

"Ours, yes. Dusty and Rainy Roller. You'll

meet them this weekend, we've already dispatched assets to retrieve and revive them," Veronica said. She smiled again at the detective.

After they left, Carrasco, with eyes as big as saucers, walked over to Lopez's cubicle: "Count me in for the road trip, dude."

The Finer Things

Off the coast of Washington state, meanwhile, evening was upon the *Blint Mary*. An inky, true dark would later set on with pea soup weather blotting out the ocean's infinite night-lights.

The vessel trailing them was a small "go-fast" boat, or "cigarette boat." Thirty minutes after it was spotted, the mystery boat vanished but that didn't mean it was gone. Nor was its presence necessarily meaningful, but, such a vessel's frequent associations with smuggling and its popularity among a trashy high-rolling jet-set crowd seemed to tighten the angles in the jaw of the ship's interim pilot. Also, this was not the Caribbean. Generally, and not surprisingly, the crew's perspective was anyone buying a cigarette boat is obviously a troublemaker because if they weren't, they would buy a nice catamaran for sailing instead, or mayhaps, a good general utility vessel for science and diving.

"That's enough to keep me interested in helping you gentlemen fish for werewolves," said the man at the till. For the remainder of the outing, Thompson, Smith, and the crew saw nothing out of the ordinary although the visibility was bad, admittedly. Most of the day's short run was spent in transit and they were back at Westport by nine.

While Becca and Veronica had taken a southwesterly detour through San Diego, some of their Bloody Roller teammates had left Phoenix directly for Washington state. After leaving off with Lopez, the two Rollers made their way to rendezvous with them in

Denver Day

Tacoma.

When one can shine anyone, literally, then trappings of want and need are easily resolved if not mooted entirely. Having all been transformed into benevolent, strongly empathetic, quazi-omniscient good-witch wolf women, the team's general philosophy and days' work were immediately and profoundly impacted. In fact, it wasn't entirely different from life changes also being forced on the worlds of Thompson and his network.

The Rollers and their Flagstaff derby counterparts, The Desert Betties, had all changed after their most recent match together, little more than a week prior. It didn't really matter if the Flagstaff team were transformed en masse by their own simultaneous deaths in a bus accident, or if it happened during some sort of coozed-up orgy with the Bloody Rollers, or if it was some sort of collective transmigration set upon all of them in due course simply as a point of natural order without fanfare or bloodshed. It didn't matter because how it became of them all was no longer philosophically or logistically pertinent. They'd become what they are, the merit of which made the past trivial and possibly interesting but not teleologically effective.

What was important now involved forward-looking perspective. Dwelling on any particular event protruding in anyone's memory would be the wrong approach, which they realized naturally by their newfound supernatural clarity of being and perception. The Rollers and the Betties all understood now perfectly, such philosophical truths about futures and pasts.

So, to get a jump on their werewolf killing, the tardy Dusty and Rainy Roller had decided, immediately after their transmigration on some dark rural Arizona highway, to travel immediately northwest. The odor and clamor of the dark werewolves was unavoidable for the sensitive, powerful, pointy ears and sovereign olfactories of the heavenly wolf women. Their innate, burning compulsion to rid the cosmology of the horrible and abominable werewolf sisters prevailed.

Rainy and Dusty reached their destination a week before Becca and Veronica. They wiped out several werewolves at a leisurely pace before being ensnared by the shark minions. Now, Becca and Veronica were en route to hook Rainy and Dusty back up to their living daylights, and also to connect with Sandy and Kitty Licker since they knew them to be sisters of a kind.

Bad Day At The Office

That night, Smith and Thompson bunked

Denver Day

at a seaside motel in expectation of returning
to the water, first thing in the morning.
After checking in, they walked to the tavern
next door. There were a few patrons,
obviously regulars, one coin-operated pool
table, a screen door, and a mellow jukebox.
The house was rife enough with seaside
culture as to be almost seaworthy in its own
right. The motif wasn't uniformly nautical,
not intentionally, but form follows function
and geography won't ever be completely
disabused. They ordered cans of lager and
sat on bar stools for an hour or so, watching
the sports news channel and speculating
about their tenuous forensic role in the
ocean. One way or another, it was a nice
diversion and they had another day to go for

their fishing expedition. If nothing turned up, they'd just go back home and pound sand on dry land. The Lickers' match on Saturday would be interesting, no matter what.

"We might have better luck hunting than fishing anyway."

"Cheers to that."

The rain continued all night, and through it the boys from Tacoma walked to the diner next to the tavern next to the motel for a red-eye breakfast. About six the following morning the detectives returned to the dock and met with the crew, the same men as the day before, and whose plans now included diving the area where the boat had been attacked, and left drifting, full of dead monsters, sharks, and fresh-hewn body parts.

Again they headed north for a couple of hours. The diving staff went to work, resurfacing after twenty minutes with good news.

Crewman Aarons: "There's all kinds of business down there. Among the lagan it looks like that cigarette boat we saw yesterday, or one just like it. It's smashed but it's a fresh wreck. Not very big or heavy and this boat has everything we need to crank what's left of her up right now. Also there's some commercial fishing gear down there; some of that tackle might be from this boat but it is hard to tell."

The crew prepared the gear for raising

the evidence, ratcheted up what was left of the little cigarette boat using the main crank, and set the little wreck down on the deck. Aarons was right, there was not much to it, little more than the engine left. Maybe it had been hit by some other, larger vessel.

They all stood there speculating about the demise of the fagboat, suspected of being the same one that tailed them for a short way the day before. Suddenly, a shock knocked all hands to the deck, as the *Blint Mary* took an unexpected, hard port-side sucker punch from a jet boat. The boat quickly began taking on water and listing, and it was soon evident, even to the landlubbing detectives, that she'd sink.

It was a good thing that everybody on

board were already wearing life vests. The three divers went to work on the lifeboat apparatus.

Some forty-five seconds after the impact, there was a gunshot, then another, and another as Smith began putting rounds from his sidearm into a werewolf that boarded the doomed boat at its point of impact. Immediately, the captain and Thompson also broke leather. The target fell but kept flopping around in some sort of a death-rattle seizure. The captain grabbed a fireman's axe from a hook at top of the deck, in the boat's muster area, and removed the werewolf's head. The creatures' flesh seemed to be rubbery and tough, as it took him several strokes to sever it. In these moments, the thought probably occurred to everyone on board, that they were in a trouble of their own borrowing. Nevertheless one brings the fight to wherever the fighting is.

A second one came over port side. Thompson quickly put five hollow points in her, and she began flopping and flagellating about the deck. The captain finished her off with his axe. Smith went to peek over the port side, then quickly ducked. He yelled back, he could see another one coming. Staying low, he moved about ten feet from his position and waited, crouching. And so they all did. Despite Smith's having moved from where he knew she might've spotted him, the thing came right over on his position, and swinging a glistening, double headed axe, she was.

He fired his sidearm four times before she got to him, but she still managed to plant the full bite of that axe, deep into his back from above him. Both the creature and Smith crumpled. The captain ran over and ended the writhing of the third werewolf. Thompson approached, and he could see, to his indescribable dismay, Smith was quickly bleeding out and pretty much already gone. The wound had split his torso nearly clean through. The *Blint Mary,* listing and sinking fast, was just about done too.

Square One

Smith was gone before they got him onto the lifeboat, where a half hour passed before the rendezvous with a Coast Guard patrol and return to Westport.

The rain still fell. The expedition was back on land by no later than four o'clock. As he changed into dry clothes, Thompson

Denver Day

was beset with an overwhelming sense of
finality regarding the ill-fated excursion. The
men went inside the office, where Thompson
filled out a form to make way for Pierce
County deputies to retrieve Smith's remains.
He telephoned Dixie with the bad news, and
instructed her to send a car for Smith.

The crew were deflated, yet still edgy,
having just had the weirdest fight they'd
probably ever had, and, they were fully
involved in the immediate shock and
frustration of the detective's killing. All were
quietly aware, after being harshly reminded,
of how quickly things can go wrong, and
that in the blink of an eye the person right
next to you or yourself can get harvested.
Another important stress factor in mind was

the presence of at-large enemy combatants in the local waters and surrounding areas.

Another murder; a vessel attacked and sunk. They are high crimes, hanging offenses. The Coast Guard scrambled all sorts of assets, air and sea, scouring the area in search of any straggling werewolf-filled cigarette boats, or anything else really at all.

Thompson felt driven to get out of there, immediately, so he did. But not without first thanking his new friends for the help escaping from the sinking ship and with the monster battle, and for transporting and holding Smith's stigmata, and their general ongoing efforts in good faith. The crew expressed their sincerest and most heartfelt regrets regarding the late detective Smith, and reassured Thompson of their availability regarding all aspects of the appropriate matters, yet also they understood why Thompson had the strong urge to bolt at that moment, even though the detective knew he would have the rest of his life to reflect upon the afternoon's events. For starters, he requested their presence at Smith's funeral, they accepted, and he hit the road.

Having found their way to the apartment by scent alone, about noon on Tuesday and concurrent with the aforementioned daytime-nightmare fiasco at sea, Veronica and Becca Roller pulled up to Sandy and Kitty Lickers' condo. The two Rollers had been in the car for more than twenty-four hours without rest, since leaving Lopez's office in San Diego. Luckily, in their newfound condition they no longer needed regular sleep, much at all.

Sandy opened the door before Veronica knocked to wave her sister-wives inside. The women had never officially met but they knew one another inside and out through a timeless soul connection. They exchanged enduring open-mouthed kisses before Sandy set them all down on her kitschy couch and fretted her Stratocaster as her new-old friends spoke.

"The dogs are loose in your neck of the woods," Veronica said. "In fact, five minutes ago, one of them killed your friend Thompson's sidekick, detective Smith."

"Yes, they are getting out of hand, eh,"
Sandy replied with a purr. "But even though
they flare up from time to time, we never
have trouble snuffing them. We'll hunt them
like the dogs they are, and force them back
into the sewers. Where they remain above
ground, or in the unlikely event they ever
walk in daylight, we'll pick them off one by
one, until their extinction. It'll be quick
work, perfectly safe."

The four subtle sisters ate a big plate of
noontime nachos, then crowded into Sandy's
dark, curtained bedroom so the Rollers could
rest from their travels. There was, however,
way more pussy-eating than sleeping in that
room, on a wet Tuesday afternoon.

A Pierce County transport arrived at

Westport to pick up Smith's body from Coast Guard custody about six that evening. Meanwhile, R. Thompson had gone straight to his apartment when he got back to town, then telephoned the lieutenant for a brief conversation. MacKinney had already gotten the bad news from Dixie.

They'd been fighting a fascinating but losing battle in recent weeks, but now it was personal and all wasn't well at this particular day's end. It was impossible for it to be. Things were changed. One of their own was lost, the scenario seemed quite hopeless. They might have been right on the mark with their hopelessness, weren't it for the Rollers' and the Lickers' looming and effective contribution to the fray.

Denver Day

The weather was dark enough to sleep but Thompson did not. He just sat back in his bed watching the classic black-and-white movie channel. His thoughts were with Smith, and Tina Santos, and the surreal past few weeks of his life. There was a knock at his door at about ten o'clock.

On The Bright Side

Thompson stood up from bed, picked up the revolver from his bedside table, and went to answer the door in his underwear. He opened it wide. Standing on the step were his girlfriends Sandy and Kitty Licker, whom he had not seen in several days. They were looking cherry as always along with two other gals Thompson didn't recognize.

"Heya Rick. Mind if we come in?" Sandy greeted him. He held the door open. She kissed him on the cheek and headed for the couch. Kitty was wearing her MC's Ale House get-up. She hugged him and showed herself to the lavatory. He welcomed the other two strange women, who Sandy

173

introduced as Becca and Veronica Roller of the Phoenix Bloody Rollers derby.

"We're very sorry to hear about Scott," Veronica said immediately. Kitty returned to the room, having changed from work clothes into a pair of jeans she'd left recently at Thompson's apartment. Sandy chimed in: "Yes dear. We're most truly provoked by your friend's late civil status, and we know you've had a long day and a long week. But also, we do have some good news."

Thompson managed a smile. "Ladies. What have you?" he asked, spirits steady.

"Well, we know exactly who did it, and why, and where they all are. And the Rollers have traveled all the way here from Phoenix, to aid us in sending these perpetrators all directly to hell," Sandy said.

"Nothing surprises me, not out of you all, not anymore," Thompson said. "I'm listening." He braced himself for a freaky answer. His expectations were duly warranted.

Kitty did the honors: "We've been holding out on you dear policeman, friend, and lover of ours. In the sense that they represent the derelict, ruined, and damned souls of our extended family tree," she said, "we have a connection with the werewolves."

At that moment, they all gently showed their souls to Thompson as Becca and Veronica had for Joe Lopez. Now the four of them glowed, purred, and strobed.

Thompson lit a cigarette. "Holy crap," he said, pleasantly shocked. "Now I understand how you're all so charming." Kitty, the closest thing Thompson had to a girlfriend, kissed him quickly, wishing to ensure he remained comfortable in light of their revealing themselves as something more, strange, and different.

"So. We can track them, and do away with them quite naturally. They've become worse than a nuisance to too many, and must be stopped," Sandy went on. "We're at your service."

"Likewise," he said. "And what of the sharks?"

"They're acting under the witching

influence of the werewolves who are hijacking their sharkfish brains in order to joy ride them around for raping and killing people, making bloody messes in public, and other wanton mischief. But the actual source of evil for that deal is the werewolves, not the sharks," Veronica said. "The hunt's still on. The shark issue should go away when we snuff the werewolves, I think."

eaus deuce fin